Text copyright © 1995 Jill Paton Walsh
Illustrations copyright © 1995 Alan Marks

First published in Great Britain in 1995
by Macdonald Young Books
61 Western Road
Hove
East Sussex
BN3 1JD

Reprinted 1996

Typeset in 15/22pt Garamond by Goodfellow & Egan Ltd, Cambridge
Printed and bound in Portugal by Ediçoes ASA

British Library Cataloguing in Publication Data available.

ISBN: 0 7500 1532 2
ISBN: 0 7500 1533 0 (pb)

Jill Paton Walsh

THOMAS
and the
TINNERS

Illustrated by Alan Marks

MACDONALD YOUNG BOOKS

Chapter One

Some while ago there was a ferryman, who earned his living rowing people to and fro across the mouth of a river, where it joined the sea. And the ferryman had a daughter who was little and light, and sang as she looked for mussels along the shore, or pinned up the linen to dry, so her father and mother called her Birdy.

Every morning of the year, except for Sundays, the bal-men and bal-maidens, who worked in the tin mine, came down to the bank of the river, and hailed Birdy's father, and he rowed the boat across to fetch them. Then they climbed the hill opposite and went to work in the mine, fetching up and finishing tin to make into shining ingots.

There was Steady Jack who held the
borer, and Hefty Jack who hit the borer
with a hammer till it made a deep hole in
the rock, and Careful Jack who packed the
gunpowder in the hole, and Fire Jack who
lit the fuse, and Standback Jack who cried
the warning, and when each had done his
part there was a flash of light, and a big
bang, and the black tin came tumbling
down from the walls of the tunnel, and
everyone shovelled and carted it away and
pulled it up with ropes and pulleys till it
came to grass.

And every man jack of the miners had a
candle stuck in a clay ball on his hatcap,
and a pair of spare candles hanging from
his buttonhole by the uncut wicks.

They all needed something to eat at
croust time, and so every morning Birdy's
mother baked nice big pasties, and Birdy
helped her fold them and crimp them into
shape. Every morning the tinners bought
them on the way by.

And then one morning when the tinners came by there was a new boy with them – a scrap of a boy, not much bigger than Birdy. Careful Jack said, "This is Prentice Jack, come to be the fetch and carry man, and help us at our tasks, and can he have a pasty too this morning?"

Prentice Jack said, "My name is Thomas, really. And I can't have a pasty that I haven't a penny to pay for."

"You'll only need a little one," said Birdy. "Have mine, and I'll bake me another, and paying will keep till your wage-day."

Thomas thanked her, and off he went, last in line up the grassy hill to the mine.

Chapter Two

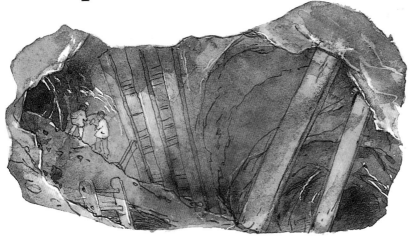

It was dark and dirty down in the mine, in
the maze of tunnels, and the holes in the
floors that dropped to darker passages
further down, and there was lots of
climbing on tippy trembling ladders up and
down, and that with baskets of heavy ore
on your back. The hammering and blasting
made your ears ring, and the dust ringed
round the bal-mens' lips and eyes and
nostrils, and made them look strangely.

Thomas didn't know what he should call things. He didn't know that a bucket of tin was called a kibbleful, and the shafts were called winzes, and the time they spent down the mine was a core, and his lunch break was croust time. People kept shouting at him and telling him things. Thomas hated it.

Just once he asked a question of his own. When all the nearby banging and hammering stopped for a moment, there was a tiny faint ringing and pattering noise, as though he could hear another team of workers faintly through the thick of the rock, or as though a battering of raindrops was ringing on a tin roof a little distance off.

"What's that?" asked Thomas, and Jack
the tribute man told him it was the fairy
miners – the Buccas – who must be working
a tiny seam somewhere nearby.

"What do they look like?" asked
Thomas.

"We don't see them; and it's only one day
in twenty we hear them, either," said Jack.
He was smiling and Thomas thought
perhaps it was a leg-pull.

"Back to work now," said Jack. It seemed to go on for ever, and Thomas couldn't believe when croust time came that it was only half-way through the day.

The men all sat on benches in one of the tunnels right where they were working, and Jack the tribute man passed the water barrel round from hand to hand, and each man unwrapped his pasty, and began to eat.

Thomas sat on the very end of the croust bench, next to the darkness, and furthest from the candles. He was so miserable that there was a channel washed clean by tears on both his dirty cheeks. He got out his own little pasty, and did it smell good!

And he had no sooner unwrapped the golden crust, and opened his mouth for the first bit, than he heard a faint little voice from somewhere beside his shoes, saying *"Not so fast! Not so hasty! Give us a bite of that there pasty! We be mortal hungry! We be a-dying down here!"*

Thomas looked down, and blow me! He saw standing there, not knee high to him, a little fellow dressed top to toe as a bal-man, with a tiny hammer in his hand, and a tiny borer tucked through his belt, and a tiny candle in his hatcap, and he was looking at Thomas's pasty with such ravenous longing on his wrinkled old face that Thomas couldn't help but feel sorry for him.

So Thomas held out the pasty for the little fellow to have the first bite, and snap! The little fellow in one bite took nearly all the pasty there was, except for the thick curve of crust with Thomas's dirty fingerprints on it. There was very little left on the crust for Thomas to nibble.

"Hey!" cried Thomas.

"I suppose you're wanting a wish," said the little fellow. "Fair enough. What will it be?"

Thomas thought how tired he was. "I wish it was time to go home!" he said.

"Sleep it out, then," said the little fellow.

The men finished eating and drinking, and picked up their tools, and there was Thomas fast asleep on the end of the bench.

"Let him be till we need him," said Jack the tribute man. "He's new to the work."

So Thomas slept through half the afternoon, and the rest of the day went more quickly than the morning, and then he could climb up the towering ladders and gain the open air, and the good green grass.

18

"How was the pasty?" asked Birdy, as the troop of tinners came down to the ferry that evening.

"It was good, but there wasn't enough," said Thomas.

"I'll make you a man-sized one tomorrow," Birdy promised him.

Chapter Three

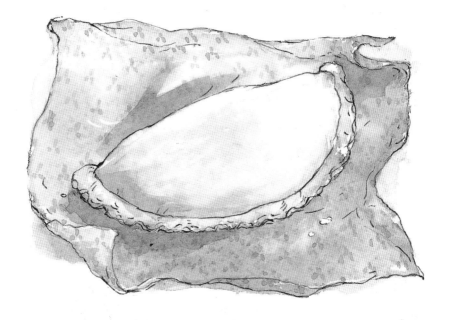

So the next day Thomas had a pasty as big as any man jack of them, and he put it in his bag, and trudged up the hill to the mine.

The work was as hard as ever, and he was just as hungry and miserable when at last it was croust time, and he sat on the end of the bench and unwrapped his pasty.

He was just about to take a bite, when he
heard again, "*Not so fast! Not so hasty! give
us a bite of that there pasty! We be mortal
hungry! We be a-dying down here!*" and
blow me! There at his side, and no higher
than the top of his knees, were two little
fellows, all kitted out as miners, and
looking so pined and hungry he couldn't
help but feel sorry for them.

So he held out the pasty to them, but he
said, "Just one bite each, mind. There has to
be something for me!"

And snip, snap, right away the two little
fellows took two tremendous bites, and the
pasty was gone right down to the dry hard
crust!

"Hey!" cried Thomas.

"He'll be wanting a wish, now," said the
little fellows to each other. "What'll it be,
Thomas?"

Thomas thought how he hated the dark.
"I'm feared of the blackness down here," he
said. "I wish I could see the daylight."

"Come come come," they said, and tugging at his shirt and trousers they dragged him away from the others, through a mazy twisty path of passageways, till they got him to a place where there was a pale disc of light on the floor, and a dusty beam standing up from it.

"Lookey up, lookey up!" they cried, and Thomas looked up, and he saw very far above him, at the top of a towering shaft, a round blue platter made of sky. It wasn't what he wanted at all, but he'd had his wish in a way, so that was that.

"How was the pasty?" Birdy asked him
as he trudged home past her door that
evening.

"It was good, but there wasn't enough,"
he told her. He was fair gnawing his
knuckles for hunger.

"I'll make you a bigger one tomorrow,"
Birdy promised him.

Chapter Four

Well, the next day Thomas's pasty was
twice as long and twice as wide as anyone
else's, and as thick as a feather pillow. He
couldn't get it into his croust-bag, and
Birdy had to wrap it in a flour sack and
sling it over his back for him. It felt good
and warm, and heavy against his back, and
the savour of it from the neck of the sack
dangling by his shoulder was mainly good!

The tinners all laughed when they saw it.
"Who are you feeding, besides us?" they
asked. "You be fair greedy for such a
runtle!"

But Thomas thought it best not to tell them, and they didn't keep teasing him long. So at croust time, when the little voice at his knee piped up, saying *"Not so fast! Not so hasty! Give us a bite of that there pasty! We be mortal hungry! We be a-dying down here!"*, Thomas cheerfully took up his great big pasty in his two hands, and held it out to the little fellow.

And blow me! All at once there was half a dozen of them, all jumping up and taking a bite, and the pasty was gone right down to the crust again, before Thomas could shout "Hey!"

"What about me?" he said, crossly.

"You get a wish," said one of the little men.

Thomas thought how hungry he felt. "I'd wish for a nice fat pasty," he said.

"Lookey see," said the first little fellow. "There's what Buccas can do and what they can't do. What they can't do is fashion food. Try again."

"I wish I worked by the sea," said Thomas, for he was thinking how the fishermen didn't have to share their pilchard pies with greedy great talking mackerel.

"Come, come, come!" cried the little fellows all at once, and they pulled and tugged at Thomas's shirt and trousers, and then fair lifted him off his feet, and rushed him away with them, feet first, round and about and always downwards, through tiny tunnels where the roof scraped the skin off his nose as they went.

Down and down they carried him, till they reached the lowest level – the adit, where the waters of the earth drained out of the mine in a dark rushing stream, stained red by the tin ore washing down in it.

The Buccas didn't stop for a minute, but waded into the rushing water, and carried Thomas along until they were at the outfall, where the adit broke out of the cliff face, and spilled all the waters into the sea.

On the very brink they put him down, with his head spinning, and there he stood, with the cliff towering above him, and plunging below him, and the sea spread out below. A gull came winging by him, and he could see a boat far out.

So Thomas had his wish, but it wasn't what he wanted at all. It was a desperately dangerous place to be standing, even if your head wasn't spinning and your heart hammering. Thomas barely looked at the sea, but went down on his knees in the water, and scrambled back up the adit, getting soaking wet as he went, and a long way it did seem! And then when he reached dry ground he had to yammer and cry, before someone came to find him, for he was very lost.

"How did you get down there for blessed sake?" Jack the tribute man asked him.

But Thomas didn't like to say. "I missed my way," he said.

Going home that evening, Thomas was so faint with hunger he could hardly walk.

Standback Jack had a word with him on the way. "It doesn't do, you'll find," he said to Thomas kindly, "to eat a hefty morsel at croust time. It weighs you down. No wonder you feel queasy. Have a modest bite, and keep your hunger for your supper time. That way you'll be nimble all day. Trust me for it."

Thomas could have wept with the unfairness of it! And here was Birdy, coming up the path to meet him, to find how he had got on. She could see at once there was something wrong.

"What's amiss, Thomas?" she asked him.

"I'm *hungry!*" he wailed at her. Well, by good luck she had a bannock in her apron pocket, made up with the scraps of the dough, that her mother had given her for her tea. Thomas wolfed it in one bite, and felt better.

"How was the pasty?" asked Birdy.

"I don't know!" cried Thomas. "There wasn't enough!"

"There's something the matter with you, Thomas!" said Birdy. "We've fed mortal many bal-men and bal-maidens twice your size and more, and they've always been staunched and pleased with the fare!"

So Thomas told her about the Buccas.

"And there wasn't any carrot left in your part?" Birdy asked him. "And there wasn't any onion? And there wasn't a morsel of tatties, or a taste of the gravy?"

"Nothing left but the crust," he told her, miserably. "And most of that had my fingerprints on it, and couldn't be eaten."

"Couldn't you tell them no?" Birdy asked him.

"You should see them, Birdy. They looked so ravened and wretched and starvling, you couldn't deny them a bite, when you've your hands full of food."

"We've got to think of something, Thomas," Birdy said, "or you'll starve to death. I'll ask my mother and father."

"We must bake him a famously larger pasty, then," said Birdy's mother.

"Doesn't do to get across a fairy miner," said Birdy's father. "And they could do with some Buccas' luck up there. The tin lode is nearly worked out, and there won't be livings for much longer."

Chapter Five

Well, the next morning, when the tinners came by, there was a wheel-barrow waiting for Thomas. And atop of the barrow was a pasty that was six foot across, and as thick as a mattress! It had taken the oven for itself, and filled the space that cooked six-dozen loaves on a normal morning. It was wrapped in a sack with a rope and pulley tied round it, ready to lower down the shaft, for it was larger by far than a lad could hope to carry.

"You be horrible greedy, Prentice Jack!" said Hefty Jack to Thomas. "You can't eat that by yourself, and that's a fact. Nobody could."

"Even the giant Tregeagle couldn't eat that much at a sitting!" said FireJack. "You should be ashamed to try on such a guzzle!"

But there wasn't much spark in their teasing – it was a bad sort of a morning.

At the top of the shaft, Jack the tribute man lined up his men, and he told them, "We've worked all the tin in our tunnels, boys, and if we don't find a new and likely lode very shortly we'll all be gone overseas before Christmas. Keep your eyes skinned for a gleam or a glint, every one of you."

Thomas was busy lowering his pasty down the shaft till he reached the place where they were working. He left it beside the water barrel, and the croust-bags of the others, and went to work. He really thought there might be a bite for him, this time.

But when the work was half done, and
they tramped back to their benches for their
croust time, a strange sight met Thomas's
eyes. There was his great pasty, propped up
on four chunks of granite, and there sitting
cross-legged round it, as though it had been
a table, were a dozen or more of the
Buccas, their napkins tucked under their
chins, and their knives and forks at the
ready.

"Yum yum yum, let's all have some!"
they cried, and as Thomas reached out to
break a piece for himself they all began to
eat, and the pasty was gone in a trice,
leaving just a seated ring of the little fellows
and heap of crust crumbs.

"Thieves! *Thieves!*" cried Thomas in a
rage. "That's my pasty you've taken! And
I'm HUNGRY!"

"You never are!" said FireJack, who was
sitting next to Thomas on the bench. "Have
you gobbled up all that vasty pasty? You'll
be ill!"

Thomas put his head in his hands. It was clear to him that none of his mates could see or hear the Buccas, that they were a torment just for him alone.

There were his team, all sitting around him. Their clothes were damp and dusty, and their faces sticky with sweat. And they were quiet and dejected today, as each man thought about leaving Cornwall behind, and going to far away lands where there might be more tin to be found, and a miner could cut a living for himself out of the hard rock.

Thomas felt a little tug on his sleeve. "Have a wish, Thomas," said the first little fellow. "We owe you a wish, and we always pay our debts."

Thomas thought how mournful his mates were feeling. "I'd like tin," he said. "Find us a likely lode – we need tin."

And to his amazement there was the little fellow shouting "Huzzah!" and dancing around like a spinning top or a boy on a birthday.

"We thought you'd never ask!" he said,
"Come come, look and see . . ." and he
began tugging Thomas along by handfuls
of his clothes, and his friends all pushing
and pulling with him.

It was only a little way they dragged and
carried Thomas, and then they set him
down in the darkness, where only the
candle in his cap shed a glimmer, and put
his hammer in his hands, and said, "Try there!"

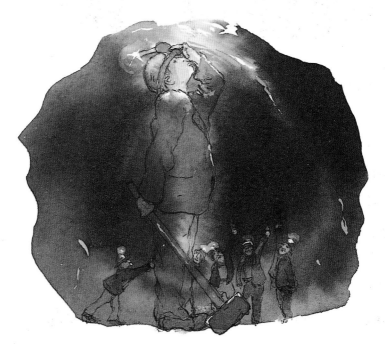

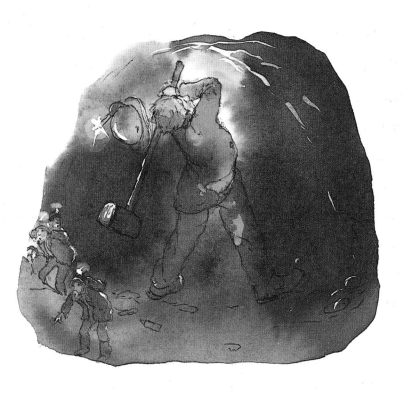

Thomas swung the hammer, and struck where the little fellow pointed, and a great tumble-down of rock fell out of the wall, and showed him behind it a tunnel, all made and ready, and in the walls of the tunnel as far as his candle-light fell the lode of tin was running, ready to cut. The little fellows didn't use gunpowder, he could see, but the bore holes were all made and ready.

"All for you, Thomas, all for you!" the Buccas were crying, and cavorting round his feet, and up and down their lovely likely lode. And as they danced they were flickering in his eyes, and turning sea-blue, and transparent as fire, until all he could see was a ring of dancing blue flames, guttering and blowing out as they moved away from him into the dark.

Thomas rubbed his eyes and went to fetch the others.

Chapter Six

There was a fair mountain of ingots made from the tin in that tunnel. Prentice Jack, that's to say, Thomas, had a due share, and a fine share it was. He and his mates stayed in Cornwall, and stayed lucky for many a year. They changed Thomas's name to Prospect Jack, because he was so good at finding tin.

And soon he didn't need to go hacking and heaving and carrying down the mine, but built himself a fine house in St Ives, and lived at ease.

But once a month, or thereabouts, he would get up early in the morning, and off he would go to the ferry. Birdy and her mother would have ready an oven-busting pasty, balanced on a barrow, and Thomas would pay for it with a golden guinea.

Then he would trundle it up the hillside, and lower it away down the mine-shaft. If anyone asked him about it his answer was pat and ready.

"I'm a man that pays my debts," he would say. "And there's some that can't fashion food, but that *loves* to get their teeth into a good Cornish pasty!"

Look out for these other titles in the Red Storybooks series:

Birdy and the Ghosties by Jill Paton Walsh
Illustrated by Alan Marks

Birdy has second sight, but has no use for her gift until the day
the ghosties arrive . . .

Matthew and the Sea Singer by Jill Paton Walsh
Illustrated by Alan Marks

Birdy buys an orphan boy for one shilling. The boy, Matthew,
has a wonderful gift: he has a voice like an angel's. But one day
Matthew goes missing. Where could the boy with the beautiful
voice have gone?

The Sea Horse by Anthony Masters
Illustrated by James Mayhew

Jamie is swimming in the sea when he gets caught by a strong
current and is in danger of drowning. Suddenly a magnificent
white horse appears and takes him safely to the shore. But then
the white horse is captured by a cruel farmer. Can Jamie rescue
him?

Fair's Fair by Leon Garfield
Illustrated by Brian Hoskin

Two vagrant children are led by a large black dog to a mysterious
house where they are amazed to find warmth and food in
abundance.

All these books and many more in the Storybooks series can be
purchased from your local bookseller. For more information about
Storybooks, write to: The Sales Department, Macdonald Young Books
Ltd, Campus 400, Maylands Avenue, Hemel Hempstead, Herts
HP2 7EZ.